W9-ATT-442

Nicholas Bentley Stoningpot III

Nicholas Bentley Stoningpot III

by Ann McGovern

illustrated by Tomie de Paola

CAROLINE HOUSE

BOYDS MILLS PRESS

Text copyright © 1982 by Ann McGovern
Illustrations copyright © 1982 by Tomie de Paola
All rights reserved

Published by Caroline House
Boyds Mills Press, Inc.
A Highlights Company
910 Church Street
Honesdale, Pennsylvania 18431
Printed in Hong Kong
Originally published by Holiday House, New York, 1982

Publisher Cataloging-in-Publication Data
McGovern, Ann.
    Nicholas Bentley Stoningpot III / by Ann McGovern ; illustrated by
Tomie de Paola.
[32] p. : col. ill. ; cm.
Originally published by Holiday House, New York, 1982.
Summary: Shipwrecked, a young boy makes a happy life for himself on a
tropical island, far away from the dull life of his wealthy parents.
ISBN 1-56397-104-6
1. Shipwrecks—Fiction—Juvenile literature. 2. Islands—Fiction—Juvenile
literature. [1. Shipwrecks—Fiction. 2. Islands—Fiction.] I. de Paola, Tomie,
ill. II. Title.
                    [E]   1992
Library of Congress Catalog Card Number: 91-77614
The text of this book is set in 14-point Times
The illustrations are transparent colored inks.
Distributed by St. Martin's Press

10 9 8 7 6 5 4 3 2

For Marty, who shares a paradise island
A. McG.

For Lon Driggers, who was preppy when
I first met him and now has his private
paradise on top of a hill
T. deP.

Nicholas Bentley Stoningpot III

was sailing the seas on a beautiful boat with his parents and their friends. All day, Nicky listened to the clink of their drinks.

His mother said, "Do you know what the baron said to the countess?"

His father said, "Did you hear what the duke did?"

And on and on and on.

The cook made Nicky special treats he could not eat. The butler brought Nicky fancy drinks he could not swallow.

The crew did exciting things. But Nicky was not allowed to be with them.

At night, they played games and told funny stories.

But Nicky had to be in bed by seven o'clock.

Nicky was bored.

"I am bored, bored, bored," he shouted to the wind.
"Bored, bored, bored," he called to the white sea birds.

"Bored, bored, bored," he cried to his parents.
But they didn't hear him over the clink of their drinks and the patter of their chatter.

Nicky longed for adventure. "Any little adventure will do," he sobbed into his satin pillowcase.

That night the wind howled. The waves tossed. The thunder cracked. The lightning lit and split the skies.

SMACK. CRACK. POW.

The big boat was sinking in the storm. The adults grabbed their diamonds and furs, and the crew sailed them away to safety in the lifeboat.

The big beautiful boat smashed to pieces. And Nicky was adrift on a piece of the smashed boat. For two days and two nights, he drifted. He was cold and wet and hungry and thirsty. And he was not alone. Big sharks and big whales swam around and around him.

On the morning of the third day, Nicky was almost a goner. He opened his eyes to take a last look at the world. What did he see but land! Beautiful land! He saw an island ringed with trees and fringed by a white, sandy beach.

The very first thing Nicky did on the island was to break open a few coconuts. He drank the sweet coconut milk. Wow, was he thirsty! He ate the white coconut meat. Boy, was he hungry!

Then Nicky looked over his island. It was truly a paradise. The sand was as soft and as powdery as sugar. The water was warm and sparkled blue-green in the bright sun. Parrots flew out of the trees to welcome him. Two wild goats came over to greet him. There was even a monkey! Best of all, there were no people. Nobody to tell him what to wear and what to say and what to do.

It was perfect.

"I'll call my island Monkey Island," Nicky said. "In honor of my new friend."

Nicky had plenty to eat—fresh fish every day and wild nuts and berries and fruit. He had plenty to drink—fresh goat's milk and coconut milk. He had plenty to do. He made a little house. He made a bed, a table, and two chairs. One chair was for the monkey. He made plates and a glass and a toothbrush.

He made a sign on the highest part of the island:

Nicky had never been so happy in all of his life.

Meanwhile, 5,000 miles away, his parents discovered he was missing. Headlines in the newspapers read:

Helicopters flew the skies looking for him. Boats roamed the seas searching for him.

And on faraway Monkey Island, Nicky found a new delight in every day.

The storm that shipwrecked Nicky wrecked other ships, too. Some of the drifting cargo made its way toward Monkey Island.

Every day, new treasures washed up on the shore. Three pairs of shoes and tattered clothes. Old feather hats and funny wigs. One day Nicky found a trunk—filled with games and books and chocolate bars.

He collected piles of treasure. Nicky grew strong from his healthy outdoor life. He grew smart from reading hard books.

One morning Nicky was awakened by shrieking parrots and crying goats. The monkey was howling and running up and down the trees. The reason for the commotion was a rescue boat, sailing closer and closer to Monkey Island.

But Nicky didn't want to be rescued. He wanted to stay right where he was—on this island, with the parrots and the goats and the monkey. Quickly he searched through his pile of treasure. He made a wonderful disguise.

Now he didn't look a bit like Nicholas Bentley Stoningpot III.
He looked like a gray-haired old lady.

The rescuers peered through their telescopes.

"There's no one on that island but a monkey, two goats, and a gray-haired old lady," they said, and they sailed away.

Nicky changed his sign.
He wrote:

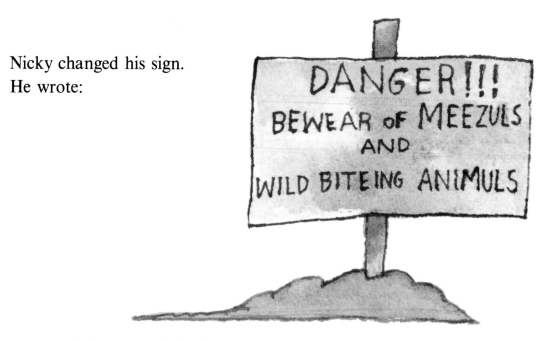

Whenever Nicky heard rescue planes in the sky or saw rescue boats in the sea, he dipped into his pile of treasure.

He fooled them all. Some days he looked like a mean, fierce pirate.

Some days he looked like a clown.

Once he looked like a wild beast.
No one thought he looked like Nicholas Bentley Stoningpot III.

After awhile, the newspapers got tired of printing stories of the billionaire's missing son. Nicky's parents spent the million-dollar reward on more diamonds and furs and another big beautiful boat.

Nicky was very happy on his island. Every day, he had new adventures. He made a fine, strong raft for sailing away. He thought one day he might want to leave Monkey Island, and go back to the real world.

But not yet.
Not for a long, long time.